HAUNTED REFLECTIONS

PART 1

Andrew J. Wilding

Copyright © 2021 by Andrew J. Wilding.

ISBN: Softcover   978-1-953537-43-0

Printed in the United States of America.

To order additional copies of this book, contact:
Martin and Bowman
1-855-921-1348
www.martinandbowman.com

SCARECROW

INTRO

This is a story about a young man trying to deal with his demons in his past, present and the future of this outcome not only will he be respected but he will be a LEGEND, even a nobody can be a somebody at the end of all things. The question is that will Scarecrow defeat his demons OR will his demons defeat HIM?

CHAPTER 1

THE BEGINNING

Before he was called Scarecrow, his real name is Jeremy Andrews. All his life he was picked on, made fun of, taken advantage of things by others, and can't do nothing right (in the eyes of people of course). Jeremy lives with his parents in a small cottage up in a farm field-that little town is called Eternal.

Eternal came from the first King of Hydra back about five hundred years ago. The reason is because of the beauty and nature of it. King Luke back then said that if he died OR was killed in battle, he would like to rest his soul in the hills of this beautiful part of Hydra for all eternity and that's where the name Eternal came from.

Jeremy Andrews worked hard with his father working on the farm and helping his mother do house cleaning as well. His parents names are Carl and Amber.

It doesn't matter how hard Jeremy worked-mornings and evenings-it wasn't good enough for them (in their own eyes). Jeremy often asked himself why they treat him like this. Maybe it is because he is good of what he likes doing for his pass time, like a hobby. His hobby is making weapons-swords, maces, axes, spears, bows and arrows (but they are all small in size). Jeremy's father Carl blew up at him more than once because of this skill Jeremy has. His father said to him many times to take the weapons he has made and sell them so he can buy some food and milk to put on the table. But Jeremy doesn't believe in violence, so if he did that, in his own mind he thought he might be encouraging the people to go out there and hurt (or maybe even kill) people.

Jeremy told his father that it was just a past-away-time hobby for him to do when he is not working on the farm or doing any housework.

His mother agrees with Carl but doesn't want to realize of what Jeremy was saying about the weapon-hurting-people thing. It was like this for Jeremy for thirty three years, until one night his mother Amber asked Jeremy to go to the waterfall and get two big buckets of water from there.

So, as usual, Jeremy went to do what his mother asked him to do. He always said to himself he can't get a break from chores (and this was after supper).

When Jeremy got to the waterfall, he saw something or SOMEONE. This meeting would change his fate and future forever-maybe be even LEGEND.

CHAPTER 2

THE STRANGER

As Jeremy drew closer to the waterfall, he saw a dark, brown hooded figure standing, staring at the waterfall. Jeremy thought he or she or WHATEVER was getting something to drink. He got closer and closer to the hooded figure and as Jeremy was about to speak, the hooded figure said to him, "I was waiting for you, Jeremy", he said.

Jeremy knew it was a he by the tone of his voice but Jeremy didn't know if the hooded figure was really a he OR something else. His voice sounded like half human/half beast. And was very surprised to hear from him that he was waiting for him. Jeremy asked him, "How do you know my name and why were you waiting for me"? he said. "Time will tell", said the hooded figure. "What is your name?" Jeremy asked. The hooded figure said, "You can call me Stranger for now", he said, "I will give you my REAL name later, you will understand". Then Jeremy said to Stranger, "So what do you want with me then", he said.

Stranger looked at him but Jeremy had a hard time trying to see what he really looked like with that hood over him. Stranger walked around Jeremy a few times and said, "This will be a shock to you but I am from the future-where King Luke is. It is at a time of fighting, power and greed. The King asked me to come to you for help-five hundred years from the past to be exact", said Stranger.

Jeremy didn't know what to think of all of this and then he answered, "What can I do to help King Luke with"? He said. Stranger replied, "You have a gift of making strong and light weapons, like no other person can do", he said.

Jeremy answered back, "How do you know I can make weapons and they can be light and strong at the same time", Stranger said, "Like I said before Jeremy Andrews, time will tell at the end of the journey. It will ALL make sense at the end of the day". Jeremy answer back, full of anger and rage, "WHAT IF I DON'T DO THIS DEED FOR YOU AND YOUR KING. WHAT IF I DECIDED NOT TO DO THIS AND JUST WALK AWAY". Stranger said in a higher pitch of tone in his voice, "If you don't do this Jeremy, the very land you stand on now, it will not be here and all the beauty, greenery, flowers and even this nice waterfall will be bone-dry. And if you don't do this deed JEREMY ANDREWS, the king said to curse you for all eternity", said Stranger as he sucked more air into his lungs and was trying very, very hard to keep his cool with Jeremy. Jeremy didn't know what to think about what Stranger said to him.

Jeremy said to Stranger, "You are a very strange man OR whatever you are Stranger, the stranger. I really think you need major mental help, I am not doing it, GOOD-BYE", replied Jeremy. As when Jeremy was walking away with his two big buckets of water, shaking his head and laughing silently, Stranger took out a small stick and said, "Crowy, crowy, curse this foul and let it be flowy, make this warm-blooded foul be cold-blooded and represent all kinds of crows".

With that Jeremy screamed in pain, dropped the buckets of water, passed out by the waterfall next to the lake and the rest was just pitched-black to Jeremy.

CHAPTER 3

THE BIRTH OF SCARECROW

When Jeremy woke up, all he saw were the eyes of Stranger looking down at him. The eyes looked green, just like his and a silly grin he gave him as well. But that is all Jeremy could see from his face. Jeremy stood up very slowly because he was in a lot (of course no help from Stranger) of pain. When Jeremy was about to say something to Stranger, he looked into the water and saw his reflection from it. Jeremy was lost for words or should I say speechless in that manner. His appearance is different, he didn't look like Jeremy at all, he more than less looked like a "SCARECROW".

His body looked very skinny, very tall, the arms looked deformed, his face very scary looking, his hair looked like hay and his shoes were no longer shoes anymore, they turned into log, brown boots.

Stranger looked at him laughing and said, "I really believe your new look is better then your old one, it represents your TRUE nature in life, like someone with no friends-no family to call your own and more importantly-NO CAREER and no one to relay on only yourself. You see Jeremy, or should I say SCARECROW (ha, ha, ha). A scarecrow is left alone, no body notices them, like the saying to a scarecrow, SCARECROW, this phrase would suit it and you would agree with me one-hundred percent. The phrase is "Being forgotten is worse than death", do you agree with me, SCARECROW", said Stranger as he begin to sit down and laugh at the creature Scarecrow who really (who used to be) is Jeremy.

Jeremy (who is now Scarecrow) turned around, stood up and stared right at Stranger with anger, full of rage and hatred and shouted at him saying, "TURN ME BACK TO NORMAL NOW, he cried. "I don't deserve this Stranger, no body does". Stranger stop for a moment, paused and said, "You are right Scarecrow, NO BODY DOES". Scarecrow answered back, "My name is not Scarecrow, my name is JEREMY ANDREWS". Stranger looked back at him again and said, "Funny, you look like a scarecrow to me, SCARECROW, HA HA HA", he said and sat back down again. Scarecrow replied, "Why did you do this to me?", Stranger answered, "I did that because you refused to help me and King Luke". Scarecrow answered back, "I have a freedom and will to do as I pleased". "You are right", said Stranger, "But not in this case, Scarecrow".

Scarecrow begin to cry by the lake. Stranger got up and walked over to Scarecrow and said, "If you go home and tell your parents what happened, they will not believe you. Your father would probably attack you with one your weapons you made in your spare time, then Carl and Amber would jump on the horse and cart, race to the king of this time, who is King Victor and he will send his knights down to investigate the problem. And if they saw you, nine chances out of ten they will kill you. So you have no choice but to help me and King

Luke and if you aid me and the king of my time, I will help you return to your normal self again. But at the end of the day, you will WANT to keep your scarecrow form, SCARECROW", said Stranger.

"And why would I want to keep this hideous form, a body that looks like it has no life at all what-so-ever". "You had no life to start with", said Stranger, "what life did you have by being a slave puppet to two people who they don't even know you are alive". "Your childhood", Stranger went on as he got angrier, "Everyday you were pick on and beat up, at one point left for DEAD". Scarecrow looked at Stranger and realized what he was saying is the truth. Stranger went on, "And when your parents picked you up and carried you home, they said to you to wash the blood off of you and start making supper. Your parents are real something, REAL something indeed, and you call that a life. If that is what you call a NORMAL LIFE, then I am the next king of Hydra". Scarecrow stood up and looked at Stranger and said, "What do you and your king want with me?", he said. Stranger said, "You already know what that is Scarecrow". "You are telling me there are no blacksmiths in your time?", said Scarecrow with both of his eyebrows riseed upward. "Not like you Scarecrow", said Stranger with a greasy grin on his face.

Scarecrow walked toward Stranger and said, "When do we leave to go see king Luke?" "As soon as you are ready", said Stranger with a silly grin still on his face. He caught hold of Scarecrows hand, took out a small stick and waved it up and down a few times, then a door appeared in front of them. Stranger opened the door, it was very dark inside. Stranger and Scarecrow walked through it and the door closed behind them.

CHAPTER 4

FIVE HUNDRED YEARS IN THE PAST

When Scarecrow stepped through into the other side of the door. His feet landed on rock, very wet and very noisy. It was the same waterfall back in his time where he always get the water for his parents (and first time encountering Stranger as well). Nothing has changed in his eyes of what Scarecrow has seen so far. When he stepped further away from the waterfall, everything was the same like Scarecrow had never left his own time. Scarecrow said, "So what is wrong in your time? I see beauty, nature, even the air is clean, like back in my time". Stranger replied, "Right now is fine but down the road of this journey there might not be any BEAUTY, NATURE, or CLEAN AIR". Scarecrow shook his head and followed Stranger to whatever path he was leading him. To everything Scarecrow has seen, why do they need him to make weapons for the king of this time? Scarecrow sees no fighting, all he can see is people helping people, with smiles on their faces and all. Of course they didn't see Scarecrow or Stranger, they were both in a distance from it all.

It seemed Scarecrow has walked for miles and miles, hours and hours. Scarecrow was just taking in all the beauty around him. The views of valleys, mountains, rivers and animals. Scarecrow said to himself that it must be serious stuff for a man or WHATEVER to travel in time to seek help from Scarecrow. Not only from Stranger but even the king of this time, King Luke of Hydra himself as well.

Just as when the sun was setting, they both came to a house-like-cottage, very old and very much alive. Stranger knocked on the door then he turned around and looked at me with that greasy smile of his.

CHAPTER 5

AN OLD FRIEND

Stranger knocked on the door, there was no answer. Stranger knocked on the door again and shouted, "Gobby, are you home? After a noise came towards the door and opened it. Not a person answered the door but a creature. Very small in height, very build-like heavy looking. He looked old, very long hair like sandy-color. His teeth looked very sharp looking like his fingers and toes, very long too. Stranger called him Gobby. Either Stranger brought me here to see this creature Gobby OR Stranger was just passing by, either way Scarecrow had no choice but to follow Stranger because Scarecrow wanted to return to his normal self again. And then Scarecrow remember Stranger saying something that at the end of the journey, I will want to look like this scarecrow figure- I wonder what he meant by that.

Anyway, Gobby answered the door, greeted Stranger and welcome him in. As for me, he just stared at me wondering who the hell is this person or creature with Stranger.

Stranger said to Gobby, "What took you so long to answer the door, my old friend"?. "I was making some bread and just put them in the oven". Then Gobby turned around, looked at me and said, "Who is this stranger, Stranger"? Stranger replied, "This young man is the CHOSEN ONE". Gobby stared and said, "REALLY, finally there is hope in Hydra after all," Gobby said.

Scarecrow answered in rage and said, "Let me guess, you cursed Gobby too because he didn't want to do your bidding as well". Stranger looked back at Scarecrow and said, "SILENCE, don't you ever disrespect my friend again. I knew Gobby when we were kids and if you EVER say anything like that again to Gobby

OR anyone else, I will give you that much pain you will wish you haven't been born". "If you do that, then who will save your precious land"? said Scarecrow. Stranger said, "I am warning you boy, my mercy has very, VERY few limits".

Gobby said, "Relax Stranger, I don't blame this young man for being angry with you, after all YOU did curse him to look like a scarecrow, right?" Stranger glared at Scarecrow and went over to help himself to some tea. Gobby added, "So what is your partners name Stranger"? "I called him Scarecrow", said Stranger with that idiotic grin on his face. Gobby said, "Well, it suits him". Gobby looked at Stranger and they both laughed that much they fell off their chairs. Scarecrow looked at them with that much hate and anger, he wished he had one of his weapons he had made to hit both of them with.

Gobby said afterwards, "As you can see myself and Stranger go way back. His real name is not Stranger, he told me to call him that so you can't call him by his real name. The reason is because Stranger is an important man in these lands and when that time comes, you will understand why he said to you and me to call my friend here, Stranger" said Gobby, as reached for his cup of tea. Scarecrow said, "This must be an important mission for Stranger to travel five hundred years in the future to bring me here". "So true, Scarecrow, so true, said Gobby". Oh, I forgot my manners, would you like a cup of tea"? Scarecrow answered, "Yes, please." Gobby poured a cup of tea and handed it to Scarecrow. "Would you like something to eat"?, Gobby added. "No thank-you", replied Scarecrow.

Gobby looked at Stranger, they both nodded their heads up and down, turned to look at Scarecrow and did the same thing. Gobby leaned over, looked right at into Scarecrow's eyes and said, "It might be hard for you now, like the way you look, the way Stranger is treating you and all. But at the end of the day Stranger will be your friend, with me included, and only you know when that day is there".

Scarecrow stared back at Gobby's black eyes, that serious look he had on him, telling Scarecrow what he was saying just might be the truth. Gobby sat back in his chair and said, "You are the hope for all of us, that means YOU". "Are you a friend of King Luke, Gobby"? said Scarecrow. Gobby turned to look at Stranger and back at me then said, "I am not but Stranger is". From that moment, both Gobby and Stranger looked very sad.

After that moment of silence, Gobby stood up and said to both Stranger and Scarecrow, "You will both remain here tonight to get some rest. I bet you both are very tired after walking all day. We shall talk tomorrow, I didn't realize it was that late. Happy good night to you both". With that Gobby went toward his bed. Stranger stood up, stared at Scarecrow and off he went to sleep on the old sofa bed. Gobby's bed looked very old as well. You had to climb a ladder to get there. Scarecrow's bed was hay on the floor. Gobby uses it to get the fire going because he has no animals around his home to call his own, that was Scarecrow's guess. Scarecrow could not think what to make of it all and it all started just to go to the waterfall to get water. And now he is encountered by a man who calls himself Stranger, turns him into a scarecrow and calls me Scarecrow, we both go back in time five hundred years in the past to save the very land he, himself, lives on. Scarecrow said to himself after thinking about all of this, "This is nuts". Stranger turned over to look at Scarecrow and said, "You think this is nuts and insane, this is just the beginning, now get your rest like Gobby said, you will need it tomorrow morning, a very busy day indeed".

Scarecrow looked at Stranger and this time he did not grin but with a serious look. Stranger turned over and went to sleep. As for Scarecrow, he turned over and just stared out the window at the bright moon while laying on the hay. He wasn't worried of what's going to happen tomorrow but what is going to happen when he returns to his time. What will the outcome bring? Will the land be the same as it was then? Will there be peace, greenery, nature, and flowing water still going to be around when he returns home? All these questions were bugging him. With all that thinking Scarecrow closed his eyes and went to sleep.

CHAPTER 6

THE JOURNEY BEGINS

When morning came, Scarecrow woke up, refreshed, energized and all. He saw Stranger and Gobby were already up. Breakfast was already to eat, eggs, bacon, toast, sausages, pancakes and even milk. Milk would be a treat for Scarecrow who drinks milk very slim now a days. Scarecrow notice one thing about Gobby, he loved to eat, the breakfast he made can speak for itself. Stranger said to Scarecrow, "Come and get some breakfast, there is lots here to eat". Scarecrow NEVER saw Stranger in a good mood before. So Scarecrow went over to join Stranger and Gobby for the meal.

After breakfast, after all the dishes were washed and put away, Stranger thanked Gobby for everything and said, "Thank-you for breakfast, my friend Gobby and I should be leaving now and see you in a bit". As we went out the door, Scarecrow thanked Gobby for last night, "Thank-you Gobby for the tea and bread last night". Gobby looked at Scarecrow and said, "So you tried my bread I see, I hope you enjoyed it". Gobby then looked at Stranger and then back at me and said, "This is the beginning of a new era, new journey, and a new path. Use it wisely!". Afterwards Scarecrow and Stranger stepped out of Gobbys house-cottage like home and said good-bye and off they went. Scarecrow asked Stranger where they are going. Stranger said, "We are going around the mountains to a village called Cherry Blossom". And off they went to the town, into the wild of the unknown.

CHAPTER 7

STRANGER REVEALED

Stranger lead the way and Scarecrow followed. Scarecrow looked back, saw Gobby at his front door and waved to Scarecrow and waved back. Gobby then went back into his house-cottage like home. Scarecrow then turned around and said to Stranger, "Where will we stay tonight"? "Out into the wild", said Stranger.

It seemed they had walked for hours and hours. All they have seen along the way was a few animals, a lot of bushes, a few trees and a lot of bugs. Stranger then said out of the blue, "I have something to discuss with you tonight when we get to Lost Woods". "OK", said Scarecrow with a puzzled look on his face. Then Scarecrow asked a question to Stranger, "What is Lost Woods"? Stranger answered, "Lost Woods is a forest with a curse. Whoever enters the forest, NEVER leaves that forest alive and a lot of times they get lost or die of hunger", said Stranger. "Outside of it looks like a forest but inside of it looks wooded, so that's why they or should I say MY KIND call it Lost Woods". "Your kind"? Said Scarecrow. Stranger stop walking, turn around to look at Scarecrow and said, "Yes, my kind. You see, they have magical powers like myself to hide their true identity. You will understand tonight-ALL OF IT partner," said Stranger with that grin he gave Scarecrow in the past. It was getting late, both Scarecrow and Stranger looked very tired and made it to the entrance of Lost Woods. "This is it, Scarecrow. We are at the entrance of Lost Woods, we shall rest here tonight. Now will you help me set up the tent and when that is finished we will both go to the river and fish-out our supper, OK"? Said Stranger.

And so Scarecrow helped Stranger with the tent and afterwards they both went to the river and went fishing. They both caught four fish, big fish indeed. Scarecrow never saw fish this big in all the times he went fishing. After fishing out their supper, Stranger and Scarecrow went back to the tent site and begin cleaning the fish and getting it ready to cook them for supper. Stranger and Scarecrow did not speak or say a word to each other during suppertime. After supper, Scarecrow cleaned up while Stranger sat back, smoking his pipe and just stared at Scarecrow. Scarecrow knew he was staring at him the whole time but didn't say anything to him about it.

Then all of a sudden Stranger spoke up and said, "What I am about to tell you is very important and one of the reasons why we are at the entrance of Lost Woods, OK"? "OK", said Scarecrow. "Where shall I begin," said Stranger, "First off, about me cursing you, I had to do that and it was not King Luke's decision to do that either". "What", said Scarecrow. "I did that because I wanted you to or should I say blend in with my friends that you will meet along the way. They hate humans and I don't blame them for it one bit. You see King Luke does not like the creatures living here in the country of Hydra because, in his eyes, they are different.

A lot of them have magical powers like I said to you before, and King Luke fears that. He wants them all killed off so it will just be humans living here and only humans", said Stranger.

"If you volunteer to do this task from the beginning of our first meeting", Stranger added, "I would have still to change your appearance like you are right now". Scarecrow said, "I am confused, there are NO creatures like Gobby or anyone like that in my time". "You are right indeed", added Stranger, "And the reason is King Luke and his men killed off every creature back then. You see Scarecrow, the people made Luke the very first King of Hydra because he promised the people he would get rid of them all because he said they have evil powers, he knows the lands like the back of his hand to find them all, even called them demons from the underworld. He even said that when there is no more room in the underworld, the evil creatures will walk among us on the earth, the very lands in the country of Hydra". Stranger took a deep breath and said, "King Luke even said he knows how to get rid of them all unless they make him king of Hydra. And so the people did-without thinking or questioning the subject. King Luke was just looking at the power at the palm of his hand, getting drunk on it. And the funny part of all, KING LUKE knew they were nice creatures from the start of it all".

Scarecrow didn't know want to make out of Strangers story. Scarecrow was in shock and completely speechless all in one. Stranger said, "That is why I went back in time to change the fate of every creature living here. That is why I came to you for help, Scarecrow. I am a human as well, the only human that the creatures living here will accept". "And what makes you special Stranger"? said Scarecrow.

Stranger stood up and took off his cloak and in front of Scarecrow there stood not a creature but a young man, almost the same age as Scarecrow. "I had to change my voice and hide my facial features in your presences Scarecrow, I didn't want to give myself away", said Stranger.

Scarecrow didn't know what to make out of all of this."What is your real name then", said Scarecrow. Stranger said, "My name is Prince Josiah, King Luke's son". "WHAT", said Scarecrow. "I am telling you the truth", said Josiah. "You see Scarecrow", said Josiah, with a sad and depressing look on his face, "I no longer speak to my father and the reason is that I disagree with everything he said about the creatures in our world. I said to my father maybe we, human beings, make peace with them and spread no violence against them. My father said that peace is for the women, NOT THEM, and that he banished me from his sight and said that I am no son of his". And you still call him FATHER, why"?, said Scarecrow.

Josiah took a deep breath and said, "I really believe he can come back, with warm feelings and not full of hatred". Josiah looked at Scarecrow and looked at the entrance of Lost Woods and said, "In Lost Woods is where our REAL journey begins, my friend. I have many friends in Lost Woods and should I say the ONLY human friend they ALL have".

"I think I understand WHY you brought me here in your time Josiah. You want me to make weapons for you and "your friends" to rise up against King Luke, your own father", said Scarecrow, as he looked at the sad expression of Josiah's face. "You have to understand my position Scarecrow, I do not want these creatures dead, including my best friend Gobby.

He is my best friend because Gobby saved my life at one time, I mentioned it to father about it at that moment and at the end of the day, here we are". "Well then", said Scarecrow, "Lets get some sleep and tomorrow, we shall get to work to change yours and the creatures fate, OUR FATE".

CHAPTER 8

ENTERING LOST WOODS

After Scarecrow said that, Josiah turned around to look at Scarecrow and hugged him, then said while tears rolled down his face, "Thank-you very much Scarecrow, I knew you would understand". And then they both went to sleep at the entrance of Lost Woods.

In the morning they both packed their tent and all their supplies, after that,they both headed off into the forest of Lost Woods, the beginning of their TRUE adventure.

Inside Lost Woods, it was dark, gloomy, and very little light shine in the forest. The trees were that thick it was not funny at all. There was one big path to walk on, a very big path. Scarecrow felt he was being watched every time he was taking a step. No sound of birds, no animals, not even berry bushes to see. Scarecrow was getting scared and he said to himself often what a depressing, sad-looking sight of trees. He never saw anything in all his life, with no life in them but very much alive indeed Scarecrow said to himself. Josiah didn't say a word from the moment we both entered Lost Woods.

In the distance, Scarecrow saw smoke and what looks like a group of people. When Scarecrow and Josiah got closer, they weren't people, they were creatures, of all kinds. Young, old, and even children running around playing ball and all.

"This is the town of Cherry Blossom", said Josiah. "At first they won't speak to strangers but when they get used to you Scarecrow, they are the best company you will ever be in, trust me", said Josiah as he and Scarecrow got into the town the creatures called Cherry Blossom. Everyone stopped what they were doing and just stared at Scarecrow.

CHAPTER 9

VILLAGE OF CHERRY BLOSSOM

It had to be close to a hundred of these creatures. Scarecrow also wonder why they called their village Cherry Blossom and right now Scarecrow understands why. Right in the middle of the village was a big white tree with big red flowers on it. They look like big cherries and all of them are all opened out or should I say blossomed out. Scarecrow never saw such beauty in all of his life, all in one tree. Compare to the other trees in the forest, this tree stood out the most. What a cold silence in the village when Scarecrow and Josiah entered the village. Josiah spoke first and it seemed he was talking to the leader of the village. Josiah never called a creature there by name. The only one he did was Gobby. Josiah walked toward Scarecrow and introduced him to the village leader and said, "This young man here is Scarecrow, he will bring balance and freedom for all of us," said Josiah. Still a cold silence from everyone. "He is the chosen one,"added Josiah, "Scarecrow here has a gift to make weapons, strong as Hydra scales and light as a feather. I traveled 500 years back in time to bring Scarecrow here to help us, to get your freedom that you rightfully deserve, we will rise up against King Luke and win a great victory. Scarecrow even told me he will help all of you. Is that right Scarecrow"? Scarecrow just stared at Josiah for the longest time, didn't know what to make out of it all.

"Is that right Scarecrow"? said Josiah for the second time saying this. Scarecrow then said, "YES, I will help you but we need more warriors, more arms and legs to fight this battle against King Luke".

With that said every creature cheered. It felt like Scarecrow freed them all from everything that they were hiding from. And for the first time in Scarecrow's life, he felt important, he even felt that he was the King of Hydra. Scarecrow smiled at them all and saw Josiah clapping along with every creature there too.

When Scarecrow said that, he was welcome with open arms and were lead to the center of the village. It looked like a meeting place by the looks of it. Inside the large cabin was a picture of Josiah and underneath the picture read, "Freedom for all creatures is near, but not so lucky for the wicked and demons who stand in our way". The village leader sat down first then all the other creatures, including Scarecrow and Josiah sat down after.

Before the village leader was getting ready to say something, Scarecrow started to think about his childhood, the bad memories he experienced as a child. Scarecrow wondered how he survived all this time and right now, he is going to save a species of creatures from extinction. Scarecrow felt very important for the moment. For the first time in his life someone will appreciate his help. And it is all thanks to Josiah.

CHAPTER 10

RECRUITMENT

Just as when the village leader was about to sit down, he said to Scarecrow, "I have a gift for you Scarecrow, not from me but from ALL of us," he said. The village leader went into his old trunk and hauled out a salt-n-pepper hat. "This hat Scarecrow is our trademark for freedom and now it is your trademark. Which means it is a symbol of hope, a symbol for all to see, a symbol that you will fulfill your bargain with us CREATURES. I or should I say a trademark for freedom for all eternity". Everyone started to clap and then Scarecrow stood up and said, "I am honored, thank-you very much village leader". Scarecrow paused for a moment and said, "Not only that this salt-n-pepper hat is a trademark for freedom for all of us but I, SCARECROW, will lead the army at the enemy gates of Hydra where King Luke sits, eats and drinks". Everyone, including Josiah, stood up and cheered, shouting the name "SCARECROW".

The village leader requested for food and drink for everyone. Scarecrow then added, "I will make you weapons and show you how to make and use them for battle. I notice you creatures have magical powers. With my talent and your powers, we will bring down King Luke and his men, then WE will have a true King of Hydra and he is standing right there among us, Josiah".

"Praise to Scarecrow, our Savior", the creatures were saying over and over. Scarecrow then looked over at Josiah, both of them grinned, hit each of their glasses together and drank.

Scarecrow-"But first we need more creatures".

Village Leader-"There are lots in the swamp and up in the mountains, Scarecrow".

Scarecrow-"How far"?

Village Leader-"The closest one is about three days away and that's to the swamp".

Scarecrow-"Send out riders to the swamp when I am finished here, Josiah and I will set out towards the mountains".

Village Leader-"Right away, Scarecrow". Scarecrow said, "One thing I do know is to make solid powerful weapons and how to use them, I will teach and after me, teach one another. The more practice you get, the better you will be in the battlefield. I will also help you not to be afraid of humans and show no fear of them", said Scarecrow.

After Scarecrow finished what he wanted to say to the creatures and the village leader, Josiah went over to Scarecrow and said, "Can you REALLY teach them all these weapons that you can make Scarecrow"? Scarecrow looked at Josiah with worry and said, "All I do is try my best and hope for the better but first, this might sound crazy to you but I heard a voice in my head saying, "Go to the abandon castle, East from here and I will guide you, I have a gift for you there that will change your life FOREVER", but both of us have to go to the mountains AFTER we have finished making the weapons". "Forget the mountains", Josiah added, "I am just curious about the gift at the abandon castle. You can make the weapons when you get back, I will ask the village leader to send riders up to the mountains to bring every creature up there down to Lost Woods, to the village of Cherry Blossom, it will not be an issue Scarecrow. Scarecrow said, "True". Josiah went over to the village leader and told him to send riders to the mountains because Scarecrow and I have business at the East. Without question, the village leader did what Josiah asked and off they went to the East, heading towards to the abandon castle.

CHAPTER 11

HISTORY ON THE ABANDON CASTLE

Scarecrow then looked at Josiah and said, "Creatures have magical powers and humans don't, how can you use magic"? Josiah said, "Gobby gave me a one shot with his magic and you already know what that is Scarecrow. It is a once in a lifetime usage of magic that only a creature can give to a non-creature", said Josiah as he grinned after saying that.

It seemed like Scarecrow and Josiah had been walking for hours. It was late but not that late. The sun was blocked by the clouds and it looked like rain up ahead. Scarecrow said to Josiah, "Do you know anything about this castle"? Josiah said, "Yes", with a sad look on his face. "What's the matter, Josiah"? said Scarecrow. "You will see when we get there Scarecrow", said Josiah, even sadder then before. With that said, there it is, big, solid and........ abandoned.

When Scarecrow entered the abandoned castle, all he could see were dead bodies, some of them were even sacrificed. Dead creatures EVERYWHERE. Scarecrow asked Josiah what had happened inside the walls of this castle. Josiah answered, "Sit down Scarecrow and I will tell you everything what has happened here, OK"? "OK", replied Scarecrow, showing a lot of sympathy toward Josiah. Josiah took a deep breathe and started. "It all started when my father, or should I say King Luke", Scarecrow then rolled his eyes when Josiah said that, "discovered that the creatures made one of there own a king and you already know him and have met the formal king, Scarecrow". "I did, then who is it"? Said Scarecrow, with that puzzled look on his face. Josiah looked at Scarecrow, gave him a grin and then said, "That formal king is Gobby."

Scarecrow stared at Josiah for the longest time after hearing this and said, "REALLY, I don't believe it". Josiah said, "You better believe it. Gobby was and STILL is the greatest king of all the creatures". Josiah saying that with a bigger grin on his face. "He was the first and last king of the creatures, no other creature made one of their own, King OR Queen since". "What happened then", said Scarecrow. "Gobby was betrayed by one of his own kind". "WHAT", said Scarecrow, with anger showing on his face. Josiah continued, "Gobby was betrayed by his brother. He grew jealous of him, with his power, his status and his popularity as well. Then King Luke and his men killed a lot of creatures that day, including Gobby's brother. The creatures fought hard with Gobby next to him but King Luke had bigger numbers so the creatures fled from the battle scene and headed towards the mountains, the swamps and YES, even Lost Woods. And the rest as you can see in history". Scarecrow looked at Josiah, put his arm around him and said, "When this battle is over, we will rebuild this castle and crown a king here once more".

CHAPTER 12

SPIRIT OF THE PAST

Scarecrow and Josiah were talking about the voice that Scarecrow heard in his head and why come to this big, abandoned castle in which it represented all the creatures in the world and the very place they have crowned there very first king which is Gobby who Scarecrow first met in this world, five-hundred years in the past. Scarecrow also learned that they build this castle as well. More importantly, the voice said to Scarecrow that there would be a gift for him to use in the fight against King Luke. What gift would that be? Scarecrow asked Josiah if the creatures gave this castle a name. Josiah said that the creatures didn't understand why you should name things and give each other names. Josiah also said that the creatures don't even know Gobby is named Gobby because Josiah gave him that name. And just that a cloud appear behind both of them, they both turned around and the cloud turned into a creature Josiah remembers quite well. Scarecrow saw Josiah's face getting redder and redder with anger. Soon the spirit spoken.

"I am a spirit of the past, about twenty years to be exact". "You coward", said Josiah. "Who is that creature"? said Scarecrow. Josiah looked back at Scarecrow and said, "That is Gobby's brother". Scarecrow looked back at the spirit and said, "So, it was you who told me to come here, at the very place where you betrayed your brother and your kind"? The spirit said, "Yes, it was I who have put that voice in your head and to come here". Josiah said, "Lets leave Scarecrow, we don't need help from a traitor like him". As both Josiah and Scarecrow were leaving, the spirit, "Myself and the dead, from the battle twenty years ago, collected enough power to help you fight against King Luke and a mighty gift to aid you as well, Scarecrow".

"REALLY", said Josiah," I am amazed and at the same time surprised they would even talk to a coward, a traitor like you". The spirit answered back, "I asked myself that same question over and over again in my head but it was I who discovered Scarecrow". Both Scarecrow and Josiah stared at each other. "I have a name", said the spirit, "My name is Hope". Josiah said, "I don't believe you". Hope said, "If you don't believe me, ask Gobby, he gave me this name". "I will", said Josiah, in disbelief.

Hope said, "You are the chosen one indeed, Scarecrow. After when I was betrayed by King Luke, I went searching for that ONE in the future. I asked all the creatures for there power to make a powerful weapon to raise up against King Luke and his men, to make up for my betrayal towards my brother and for the rest of the creatures. I told them about traveling into the future to find HIM or HER, then I found Jeremy Andrews, a gift in making strong, light weapons. When I found him, I told everyone else about it in the afterlife and then I told my brother Gobby. He was just as mad as you were Josiah but when Gobby listened to what I had to say. I showed him all the power I had collected from the others, Gobby believed me. So Gobby suggested that YOU, Josiah, to go and bring Scarecrow here to our time. It has to be someone living to do it, not a spirit. And the rest is history Josiah and Scarecrow. NOW, do you believe me"? Both Josiah and Scarecrow nodded their heads up and down. "OK, now lets get to work, we have so much to do and learn about the gift I have for you Scarecrow", said Hope.

CHAPTER 13

SCARECROW REBORN

Hope handed Scarecrow a sword and said, "Scarecrow, this weapon was made in the afterlife, with ALL the creatures power combined. This sword is no ordinary sword, it can create life, at your command". "REALLY", said Scarecrow. "Yes", said Hope, "But in order for you to create life you have to give them each a soul and in order to do that you have to drive the sword into your body and the sword will collect half of your soul into it. It will not hurt at all, trust me. OH, I forgot to tell you that the creatures in the afterlife named the sword "Flame of Creation", now drive that sword as hard as you can. Josiah said in a low voice to Hope, "Are you sure it is safe, I don't know about this". "Trust me", said Hope. So Scarecrow hold the sword up high and drive it through his belly and over from the other side. At that moment, Scarecrow was covered in a black and red cloud, screaming in pain, and about a few minutes later, the cloud disappeared and Scarecrow was no longer Scarecrow anymore, he had changed.

Scarecrow was huge. Very tall, muscled out, his face changed, eyes changed, even his hat. His facial features looked more scarier then ever, his teeth is razor sharp, pointy ears. His eyes used to be green now they are dark yellow. His hair did look like hay, now it is dark black. Even his hat changed, it look like a jesters hat with three horns hanging down with bells on it. Scarecrow felt invincible by the way Josiah and Hope looked at him.

The Flame of Creation has changed as well. It looked like a black and red flame covering the sword and strings of grey going around the sword too. Josiah and Hope looked at each other and Hope said, "This is bad Josiah, someone has tampered with the sword". "Who"? Said Josiah. "I don't know but I will find out in the afterlife.

And before Hope was about to return to the afterlife to look for answers, Scarecrow took the "Flame of Creation", drove it right through Hopes soul. With that Hope screamed and exploded, like gun power into thin air. Then Scarecrow looked over at Josiah and said, "Get those losers out of Lost Woods and then run to your daddy. Tell that so-called King Luke what went down here, from meeting me up until NOW. I will created an army so GREAT, YOU and the CREATURES, even your own DADDY would probably take yourself 's out, HA HA HA. I will march to the gates of Hydra with 10 thousand warriors, that is what the "Flame of Creation" has allowed. I am telling you this not out of the goodness of my black heart but the gift Hope has given me. Now GET LOST POWERLESS ONE, HA, HA, HA, HA, HA".

Josiah scared and frightened, he ran out of the abandoned castle. While running, Josiah could hear Scarecrow laugh, a very scary, horrible laugh.

NEW INTRO

From here on end, there will be two different parts as the story ends. One is Scarecrow, behind the scenes, and the second one is Josiah, behind the scenes. Until they meet again, one last time in the battlefield which will go down in the history books for all time.

CHAPTER 14

JOSIAH-LOST WOODS

Josiah ran as fast as he could, faraway from the NEW Scarecrow. He looked behind him and stopped running, caught his breath and said, "What in the world happened to Scarecrow? Hope said that someone tampered with the sword, tricked Hope and the rest of the creatures in the afterlife. We are in seriously trouble. Not only does Scarecrow have the power to kill the dead but to bring Scarecrow here from the very beginning was a mistake like someone set Scarecrow up from the beginning but who? But Hope said also that Scarecrow is the Chosen One? But first I have to get to Lost

Woods and tell the others what has happened at the abandoned castle and then my father, I just hope he will listen to my story".

And off Josiah went running again. When Josiah got to Lost Woods and entered the village of Cherry Blossom, he saw every creature there celebrating. Josiah again caught his breath from all the running and said, "Everyone stop", but none of them heard him because of all the noise the creatures were making. Josiah said it again, "EVERYONE STOP". With that every creature, complete silence.

The village leader and everyone else looked at Josiah with concern. By the look on Josiah's face everyone knew something was wrong, terribly wrong. The village leader said, "Are you alright Josiah? Where is Lord Scarecrow? Is he alright"? Josiah said, "I am afraid Scarecrow is NOT alright and as for the title "LORD" on his name, he does not deserve it, not one bit". Everyone and the village leader just stared and looked confused. Josiah said to the village leader, "Did you get everyone from the swamps and the mountains"? "Yes, we did, all of them. Including the valleys and the hilltops". Josiah said, "That is great because we are going to need

EVERYONE". "Why", said the village leader, "Is King Luke going to attack us soon"?

Josiah said, "No. The very man OR creature OR WHATEVER, the CHOSEN ONE, is our enemy for the time being. Scarecrow has incredible power but also has the skills to make powerful weapons as well. We have to march to the Kingdom of Hydra and seek help from my father". "If we go there we will be killed for sure. You know what King Luke thinks of us and what he has done to us in the past, about 20 years ago", said the village leader. Josiah said, "I will enter first, tell my father the entire story just like I am about to tell you and everyone here".

So Josiah told the story from beginning up until now. The village leader and everyone else in the area were shocked to hear the story. "So Hope was trying to help us, PRAISE HOPE", said the village leader and every creature did. Josiah grinned and said, "We should leave at once for the Kingdom of Hydra".And off they went, a very large number of them, about 500 of them. Josiah said, "I think more is at play here". "I agree", said the village leader.

CHAPTER 15

SCARECROW-HALF HUMAN/ HALF CREATURE MAKING

Meanwhile, at the abandoned castle, Scarecrow started to dig a hole, just outside the castle gates. When the hole was big enough, Scarecrow started to pour water into it. Then a lot of soft soil and began to stir it with a big branch. When the water and soil was nice and thick, Scarecrow said, "This very mud will be my PEOPLE, my NEW ARMY". Then Scarecrow got out his sword, the "Flame of Creation",and put it downward, straight right in the middle in the hole. "HA, HA, HA, now I will begin the process in making them".

The big hole, full of mud, started to change, the same colors like the "Flame of Creation", black-red-and grey. Scarecrow laughed and said, "Everyone of them will look like me, ME, a trademark of an new era, HA, HA, HA. OH, FLAME OF CREATION, MAKE MY PEOPLE, MY ARMY, OUR FUTURE, INVINCIBLE,

HA, HA, HA". And with a few minutes later, Scarecrow's minions started to come out of the hole. Lots of them.

When they stopped coming out of the muddy hole, Scarecrow counted his minions and then looked back into the hole, "Only fifty minions and the mud in the hole is empty, I guess I have to make a BIGGER hole". Scarecrow waved his sword at his minions and commanded them to dig a much bigger hole, only forty of them, the other ten he commanded them to make clothes so they can clothed themselves. Without question, ALL of them did what Scarecrow asked them to do.

With a big smile on his face and after said to himself, "I thought of a new name for myself, how about KING SCARECROW, HA, HA, HA". As he laughed, his minions were busy digging and making clothes, Scarecrow said out loud, "THIS COUNTRY WILL BE MINE, ALL MINE, HA, HA, HA", with that horrible, cruel, evil smile of his.

CHAPTER 16

JOSIAH-INTO THE WILD

As everyone started to leave, full of anger towards Scarecrow and even Josiah. The village leader said, "I thought you said Scarecrow was the Chosen One"? "I thought he was too", said Josiah, even madder then the rest of the creatures. Along the way they met another group of creatures. The leader of that group said, "Why such a large number of you? Where are you going? It looks like all of you are going to war or something. Anyway, it is nice to see you again Prince Josiah". "Likewise, my friend", said Josiah as he went over and hugged the leader of that large group of creatures.

So Josiah told the leader of the second group everything from the beginning up until now. The leader said he heard something about every creature had to meet at Lost Woods, it was a matter of life and death but he heard NOTHING of what Josiah had told him.

Everyone was tired from walking all day so they all decided to camp out that night. When Josiah was about to go to sleep, one of the creatures came to Josiah and said, "You have a visitor, my Prince". Surprised and tired at the same time, Josiah sat up. It was one of the town's people from the Kingdom of Hydra, he looked like a hunter. The hunter said, "My Prince". "Sir", said Josiah. "I saw you with the creatures in a distance, are you and the creatures going to attack your father, your Kingdom?, said the hunter. Josiah laughed, "No, my friend I am not. Actually all of us are going to see my father with very important information, it concerns us ALL". The hunter said, "I am not a fan of the creatures, my Prince, but when I saw you with them I took a chance to speak with one of the creatures and he let me here to speak with you, if you were wondering why a human, like me, is here in a camp full of them. Is there anything you want me to do for you, my Prince"? "Yes", said Josiah, "Go to my father and tell him what I have just told you earlier, war is near, VERY NEAR and the enemy is like no other". With that the hunter said, "I shall leave at once, my Prince". "Thank-you", said Josiah. When the hunter left, Josiah went to sleep, trying to forget what had happened at the abandoned castle.

CHAPTER 17

SCARECROW-THE ABANDON CASTLE REBUILD

Still making his army from the very earth with water and soil, added in a much bigger hole (same hole) and with the power of the "Flame of Creation", Scarecrow started to think about the abandoned castle, the very birth place of his minions, his army, his new-found-family. Scarecrow has a least (right now) a thousand half human/half creatures made. "I should give you all a name", said Scarecrow, "how about Grave Diggers". Everyone cheered and crowed. Scarecrow was loving every minute of it. "Now", said Scarecrow, "How about we rebuild this castle, a trademark of our future success. And

I have the PERFECT name for this castle too. I shall call this castle the Kingdom of Creation. I shall name it after the "Flame of Creation", I think it has a good ring to it, after all I did create all of you Grave Diggers. Scarecrow stared at his new family of minions and said, "I WILL CREATE A NEW PLACE FOR US ALL IN THE FUTURE, ALL OF US AND NO ONE ELSE, HA, HA, HA".

Every Grave Digger cheered and repeated, "KING SCARECROW, OUR NEW KING, LEADER, CREATOR, AND GOD". "When we knock down the gates at the Kingdom of Hydra, we will have two kingdoms in our possession, we will rule this country and this world with an iron fist, WE WILL BE DEATH IN THEIR EYES, SPREAD FEAR ALL ACROSS THE COUNTRY, HA, HA, HA".

Every Grave Digger cheered and celebrated. After everyone of the Grave Diggers went back to work, making more Grave Diggers, clothing, and rebuilding the castle right away. Cutting down trees, putting them into piles and collecting a lot of rocks as well. "I will show no mercy for King Luke, Josiah and every creature", Scarecrow said to himself.

CHAPTER 18

JOSIAH-AT THE GATES OF THE KINGDOM OF HYDRA

When morning came, the village leader went up to Josiah and said, "I heard you had a visitor last night, someone from the town of Hydra"? "Yes", said Josiah, "I asked him to tell my father that myself and the rest of us are coming to see him, to deliver an important message, I didn't tell him anything of what had happened". "Why"? Said the village leader. Josiah said, "Because I didn't want everyone in the town and in the castle to panic". "Make sense",said the village leader. "Anyway we shall make our way to the gates of the Kingdom of

Hydra and hopefully this time my father will listen".

Josiah said to himself while walking with the other creatures, "If only my father would have listened to me, that the creatures are friendly folk, none of this would have never happened". A few miles up the road, everyone including Josiah saw someone riding a horse towards them, coming in very fast. It was the hunter that Josiah had spoken to that night. When he approached Josiah, the hunter said to him, "You must turn back quickly", with fear on his face. "Why"? said Josiah, "Did you give my father the message"? "I did", said the hunter, "But King Luke didn't believe me and NOW if you did come, right now King Luke got his men at the city gates, heavily armed". Every creature said that they should return but Josiah said, "Return to what and where? Everyone, including myself will march up to the city gates, I will go inside alone and speak to my father". So with that said, everyone marched about two hours until they reached the gates (but the creatures stayed back a distance away because they knew the people in the kingdom feared them and didn't want any trouble). The hunter was right, there were soldiers there, heavily armed. "I need to speak to my father, King Luke, it is a matter of life and death. We are not armed and as you can see the creatures are in a distance, they are no harm to no one, just myself will enter and no one else, please", said Josiah. With that, the soldiers guarding the city gates let Josiah in. "I hope my father will listen", Josiah said under his tongue.

CHAPTER 19

SCARECROW-WEAPON MAKING

It took no time to build the new Kingdom of Creation with ten thousand Grave Diggers. Now it is time to make the weapons for the army of Creation. Making weapons was Scarecrow's speciality. You put a weapon in front of him and he will make it exactly like it but a lot stronger and light as a feather.

All the weapons, even armor, helmets and shields, all stored in Scarecrow's head. "Before we begin to make the weapons and everything else, I will show you how to make them ALL. I will take longer if, Yours Truly, did this all by myself. We shall start with the basics, all the way to making the perfect weapons, armor, helmets and shields, OK"? "YES, KING SCARECROW", said very Grave Digger present. Scarecrow first got a fire going and started the materials from scratch. Every Grave Digger did what Scarecrow did and soon after everyone was making very strong, light weapons, helmets, armor and shields. The weapons were all kinds like swords, maces, axes, clubs, spears, knives, and bow-and-arrows.

Scarecrow was loving every minute of this moment. "Don't be shy Grave Diggers, make lots, LOTS, HA, HA, HA", said Scarecrow and everyone answered, "YES, YOUR MAJESTY".

Soon after Scarecrow went to his throne and poured himself some wine and said to himself, "The Grave Diggers can certainly make great wine, HA, HA, HA". Scarecrow wasn't drunk with the wine, he was drunk with POWER.

CHAPTER 20

JOSIAH-INSIDE THE KINGDOM OF HYDRA

When Josiah enter the village part of the Kingdom of Hydra, everyone stopped and stared. "There is more cheer in a graveyard," Josiah said to himself. Nothing has changed in the last twenty years, nothing at all. Just after Josiah went around the corner of the village and headed toward the castle, Josiah saw his father, King Luke, waiting at the front doors with eight soldiers by his side.

"Twenty years ago you were fat and now twenty years later you are still the same butterball", said Josiah. "You watch your mouth, you brat", said King Luke, "You came all the way here, out of your mushroom with your minion friends, just to insult me. Twenty years ago I abandoned you NOW you are here again, OH, JOY". "SILENCE", said Josiah, "If you want to disown me, FINE, but war is at your front doorstep". "Yes, I have noticed your friends outside", said King Luke. "No, not the creatures, they are here to help you fight against a force, an EVIL FORCE", said Josiah. King Luke said, "HA, HA, HA, you're funny. What do you think your mother would have said about all of this". "She would have agreed with me. And you know what, as a matter of fact mother and Gobby were close friends. I believe that's one of the reasons why you attacked Gobby's castle and killed a lot of his kind as well, that is why mother is dead now because she was trying to beat some sense into you and where is she NOW, she is dead, defending the creatures freedom". "You shut your mouth or I will knock your head off your shoulders, YOU HEAR ME, I am your KING", said King Luke. "Well, if you are not going to help us then I take my leave, KING", said Josiah.

Just as Josiah was leaving, King Luke said, "You are right you know, your mother Sandra and Gobby were close. If I could turn back time and change the past, I would. Yes, Gobby's brother was jealous of him and at the time that was a door opener for me to strike on the creatures. I guess I was jealous of your mothers relationship with Gobby and the creatures. But I will not dishonor your mother, my wife, my soul mate". Josiah turned around, smiled and said, "I missed you too father".Then they hugged each other. Josiah said after, "I will let every creature know that they are allowed to enter the Kingdom and then I will tell you the whole story from the beginning up until now". "OK", said King Luke.

CHAPTER 21

SCARECROW-MAKING PLANS FOR BATTLE- PART 1

Scarecrow with ten thousand Grave Diggers at his command and ready to spill a lot of blood for their king. Now there was one thing left for Scarecrow to do was to plan the attack on the Kingdom of Hydra.

Every Grave Digger sat down, complete silence while Scarecrow stood up and began to tell each and every one of his minions his plans. "First", said Scarecrow, "We shall surround the entire Kingdom so no one leaves alive. Size-up the environment and surroundings to see what weapons they are going to use against us. Second, everyone at the front with their shields up to block the archers arrows, if they have any. Third, the Grave Diggers armed with bows-and-arrows work together at the left, right, and rear sides of the army of Creation. Fourth, every Grave Digger armed with clubs, destroy the enemies shields. Fifth, every Grave Digger armed with axes, try to kill the soldiers with no shields and LAST, everyone Grave Digger armed with spears, maces and knives, throw them at the enemies in a distance back, but remember the knives are great for close encounters".

Scarecrow looked at every Grave Digger and said, "That concludes the plans for battle, but as for, your King, I will deal with King Luke and Josiah". With that said, every Grave Digger cheered and repeated saying, "KING SCARECROW, OUR GOD". Scarecrow grinned and looked at his army again and said to himself, "I am truly blessed, ha, ha, ha".

CHAPTER 22

JOSIAH-MAKING PLANS FOR BATTLE- PART 2

As all the creatures were entering the village part of the Kingdom, everyone looked scared. The village leader asked the other creatures to give the people peace offerings to ease the tension and they thought it was a good idea and they did. Soon after, everyone started to talk to each other. Josiah and King Luke smiled as both humans and creatures were interacting well with each other.

"Now", said Josiah, "I will tell you everything, EVERYTHING". So Josiah, the village leader from Lost Woods, the leader of the tribal group and King Luke went to the castle. Josiah started to tell his father the entire story from the beginning where he met Scarecrow up until now. After Josiah finished telling the story to his father, King Luke said, "So let me get this straight, you went back in time, with the creatures power, with the help of Hope, brought Jeremy Andrews A.K.A. Scarecrow back here in our time so you can make peace offerings to me by getting Scarecrow to make powerful weapons. And if I did not except them from you, you would have fought us to understand your situation, RIGHT". "That is right", said Josiah, "But the plan backfired, after he drove the "Flame of Creation" into himself, he more or less transformed, a different Scarecrow. Hope said the sword was tampered with by someone and it had to be someone in the afterlife". King Luke paused and said, "But he has no army, right"? Josiah looked at his father and said, "Scarecrow told me he was going to sent ten thousand soldiers to the kingdom gates but I have no idea were he is going to get a number like that". "You did say Scarecrow can create soldiers with the "Flame of Creation", right"? Josiah paused and said, "That is what Hope said BEFORE Scarecrow drove the sword into himself ".

King Luke said, "Just as a pre-caution, I will have archers EVERYWHERE, I have at least one thousand soldiers, very well trained. We will set up traps on the battlefield, we will make holes in the ground and fill them with razor-sharp spikes. And IF he does have an army, they will fall and if WE fall, I will make it sure its remembered". Josiah, the village leader, and the tribal leader nodded their heads. "No time to waste, we must act fast, NOW", said King Luke.

CHAPTER 23

WARNING FROM GOBBY

Preparations were about to begin until the tribal leader came running in saying, "King Luke, Josiah, Gobby has arrived here and he told me to tell you he has important information to tell both of you. King Luke and Josiah just looked at each other in surprise. "Bring Gobby in here right away", said King Luke. "Yes, your Majesty, right away", said the tribal leader. When Gobby entered the main chambers of the hall, King Luke went over to Gobby and said, "Before you speak, I just wanted to tell you that I am so sorry for what happen twenty years ago and when this war is over, I will rebuild your castle for you and then you can take your rightful place at the throne, it will represent all the creatures in the world".

Gobby said, "Thank-you King Luke but I think someone or SOMETHING has already rebuild it and he called it the Kingdom of Creation. Also, Scarecrow has ten thousand strong-at-least to follow his every command, even to death". Shortly after, the village leader came in, the tribal leader told the village leader what Gobby had said. Everyone was in shock, don't know what to make out of what Gobby had told them all.

"There is more, so please, sit down and I will tell you everything", said Gobby, with worry on his face. "When I heard that Josiah and Scarecrow were headed to the abandoned castle, I decided to go there and talk to both of you. When I arrived at the abandoned castle from a distance, I saw a NEW Scarecrow, making his army with the sword called "Flame of Creation. Scarecrow used that sword combined with earth, soil and water, mixed it all together like mud".

"Before you continue Gobby", said Josiah, "There is something I have to tell you". "What is it Josiah"? Said Gobby. "After Scarecrow drove the "Flame of Creation" into him, he then struck Hope with the sword after and killed him, I am so sorry", said Josiah

Gobby paused and then said, "I already know, a couple of the spirits in the afterlife told me". There was a long silence in the chambers in the great hall. "I have to tell you the rest of what I have seen at the Kingdom of Creation". "OK", said Josiah.

"Scarecrow's soul is in each of his minions called Grave Diggers which they all look like Scarecrow. In order to beat Scarecrow, you have to drive the "Flame of Creation" into his body OR into someone else. If it is Scarecrow, the Grave Diggers will ALL die OR if you drive the "Flame of Creation" into someone else, the Grave Diggers will follow that person or creature". Gobby paused and said, "Scarecrow and his minions made a lot of weapons, STRONG WEAPONS of all kinds-swords, maces, axes. clubs, spears, knives and, bows-and-arrows too. Scarecrow will be here in five days". King Luke got up and said, "We all have a lot of work that needs doing, lets start right away and show that coward what WE are made of and not of Mud either". Josiah, the village leader, the tribal and Gobby all laughed at what King Luke just said.

CHAPTER 24

JOSIAH-GETTING READY FOR BATTLE-PART 1

Four days later.....King Luke said out of the blue and white as a ghost, "They will come and kill every woman and child, what evil". Josiah, Gobby, the village leader and the tribal leader just stared at each other and back at King Luke. "There is no point in fighting Scarecrow, he already won the war, it is only facts, just think about it". Josiah said, "If we are going to lose this war, Scarecrow is going to fight for his life, we won't go down easily. We have courage, love and hope on our side". With that King Luke said, "You are right son. When the time comes you will make a damn great King when I am gone".

King Luke said as he took out his sword, "We have a war to fight, and victory is near". As King Luke walked out of the castle and said to the people and every creature present there, "I asked every creature, every strong lad to use your swords, I ask everyone of you to defend your country and your names will be remember for all ETERNITY. COURAGE, LOVE, and HOPE are very powerful weapons, USE THEM.

Everyone cheered and then they all went to the armory to get fitted out, both humans and creatures. All of them, swords at hand, shields, helmets and armor. Also carrying the flag, a symbol of the Kingdom of Hydra. The flag looked like a giant Hydra eating its enemies. All the traps were set and everyone took there positions, archers ready on top of the castle walls and the sides too.

King Luke said to Gobby, "Gobby, a rough guess, when do you think Scarecrow will be here"? Gobby answered, "My guess would be between five to seven hours, your Majesty". Afterward, Josiah said to his father in a low tone, "I always wanted to fight side-by-side with you father". "Me too", said King Luke, with a smile on his face.

CHAPTER 25

SCARECROW-GETTING READY FOR BATTLE- PART 2

Scarecrow and his minions were a few hours away from the gates of Hydra and commanded the Graves Diggers to stop marching because Scarecrow had something to say to them all. Scarecrow stood up on a platform, he was wearing solid gold armor mixed with silver with his face in the middle of it. The same with his helmet, shield and even the "Flame of Creation"at hand with his horrible face on the handle of the sword. The same with all of the Grave Diggers, Scarecrow's face was on EVERYTHING, shields, helmets, every handle of the weapons the Grave Diggers had at hand.

On the platform in which the Grave Diggers were carrying Scarecrow and said to everyone, "My fellow children, people of a new age, warriors that will make history, a power is raising and we have to show them who the REAL ruler is in the country of Hydra and in the world". Scarecrow paused, looking at his great army, with every Grave Digger in complete silence. "I am your Creator and you are the Creation, don't fail me and don't fail yourself. I trained all of you well, you are not fighters, you are WARRIORS, not weaklings like the ones we are going to destroy. I am your GOD, your CREATOR for all ETERNITY. Show those cowards what you are made of ". With that horrible smile of his Scarecrow said afterwards, "We shall march to the Kingdom of Hydra, we will leave non alive, TO WAR". Every Grave Digger cheered and hitting the ground so hard it felt like an earthquake. Scarecrow got off the platform and walked through the crowd and made his way to the front of the pack. Then Scarecrow raised the "Flame of Creation" in his hand and said, "This very blade will stain the very blood of King Luke, his precious son Josiah and even that former king of the creatures Gobby". As everyone pressed on marching, Scarecrow said to himself in a low tone, "I hope you enjoyed the view, you coward Gobby". The Kingdom Of Creation is emptied out, leaving the no-life, pale looking castle behind. All together it would take about five days to reach the Kingdom of Hydra to where Scarecrow's castle is. On this day, Scarecrow was about to make history, a war like no other, and it will be the talk for all time.

CHAPTER 26

GOBBY'S SURPRISE FOR SCARECROW

As everyone waited for Scarecrow and his minions to arrive at the gates, all the creatures were making finishing touches on the traps they had set up on the battlefield. After, Gobby walked up to Josiah and the King Luke, looked at both of them with a grin and said, "There is a reason why the creatures called this country "HYDRA". Josiah and King Luke looked at each other, puzzled. Gobby continued, "The founders of that name are called Mermen. They live in the water most of the time and the name "Hydra", to them, means water. They are on their way here and you will know when they get here". "When will they be here"? said Josiah. "Very soon", said Gobby. "The Mermen", Gobby added, "They look like half human/half fish. And in their world, "Hydra is like a guardian, like a God of the planet and there are many of them too. I think there is about, a good twenty-five hundred of them, I think". "That's great", said King Luke, "We need all the help we can get but how come I didn't know about this before, about the Mermen"? "Because", said, Gobby, "Humans back then were afraid of us, they didn't interact with us so how could they know? Your wife Sandra knew about them but never met them". King Luke turned red in the face after hearing that.

Soon after a army came from the mountain side and there they were, the Mermen, armed with tridents, wearing armor helmets and shields. "I think we are going to surprise the so-called "King", said Gobby. "You are a true friend Gobby or should I say KING Gobby. Hydra is the guardian to the Mermen and YOU are the guardian of all creatures and I am honored to have you by my side in this war. If I die I hope you and father continue", said Josiah. "Same here", said Gobby.

In the distance they could hear Scarecrows army, while the Mermen were still coming down from the mountain side and placing their positions at the city gates.

CHAPTER 27

WAITING FOR SCARECROW

"What a view", said Josiah, as everyone gather at the city gates. Scarecrow's army looked like one big, huge, black cloud with tiny lights in them (they had to be the torch bearers). "EVERYONE, READY YOURSELVES FOR BATTLE", shouted King Luke as he drew out his sword.

Gobby said to Josiah, "Your friends are with you Josiah, we trusted you in the past and even NOW". "The same here", said Josiah, as Scarecrow's army was getting even closer to the gates of Hydra. At the front of the pack of the

Grave Diggers, everyone saw a huge, mammoth, build figure leading the army, it was Scarecrow.

Everyone creature, every soldier, and YES, even the Mermen started to get scared. Josiah saw this and went to the very front and then said, "Everyone, hold your ground, hold your ground. I can see in your eyes, the same fear that will take the heart of me. But it is not this day, today we will unite as ONE, destroy the enemy, earn peace and freedom that we so rightfully deserve. We will show no mercy, no fear for this demon. We will win by courage, love and hope. This day will be a sore day but not for us, for THEM".

With that everyone cheered. King Luke went over to Josiah after and said to him, "I am honored to have a son like you". "Likewise", said Josiah. Josiah added, "Draw your swords and show no mercy, lets show this coward what we are made of, not just mud either, but REAL blood".

Everyone started hitting their shields as Scarecrow made the final steps to the city gates in the distance. The noise stopped. Scarecrow stopped and stared at Josiah. "So it begins old buddy, ha ha ha, said Scarecrow, talking low to himself.

CHAPTER 28

SPEECH BEFORE THE BATTLE

Scarecrow continued to stare at Josiah and Gobby. After Scarecrow said, "Is this it"? A group of un-experienced so-called warriors and a handful of fishes. I heard about your kind, OH YES, I also heard about that weapon you all use, that TRIDENT. I really think you all should go back to the water, your gills might dry out, ha, ha, ha". Josiah said, "What we have here are WARRIORS, not some water-soil-mud freaks you have over there". Scarecrow paused and said, "I have ten thousand at my command, you have less then half. You are outnumbered old buddy, SURRENDER". "NEVER", said Josiah,

"All I see is that your minions are going to enter their doom because of ONE-MANS-GREED". Scarecrow answered back, "Careful boy, my mercy has limits and for saying that, every man, woman, child, creature and Merman shall DIE". Josiah then just glared at Scarecrow.

Scarecrow took his sword, the "Flame of Creation" and said, "On my challenge, in ancient laws of combat, we are met on this chosen ground, for good and all, who will be the rulers of Hydra and this planet, us natives, born right wise while the defiling hoards defiled over it". Every Grave Digger started to cheer and hitting their shields. "Well then, in your ancient laws of combat I accept your challenge to the so-called natives. You plague our people with evil but no more, we will rise again and calm these lands and freedom for ourselves". Every Merman, creature and the rest of the people cheered. "After Scarecrow said, "Well, let the "Flame of Creation" guide my hand and rise against your Hydra-weakling protectors". "You will receive the true power from all of us and the Hydra together", said Josiah. With all that said, both armies clashed into each other. The war started. The biggest and greatest one ever, is about to go down in the history books, in the country of Hydra, for all time to come.

CHAPTER 29

FULL OUT WAR

When it came to numbers, Scarecrow's army had the most but Josiah's army was doing more damage. On Josiah's side, the knights were busy blocking attacks, arrows and also attacking back with one big, huge attack then group back quickly for defense. The archers were doing a great job on the mountain side and on top of the castle too. They were going a great job as well blocking the arrows from the Grave Diggers and killing a lot of them off in the process. The village people, same as the knights, they followed their lead and tried to do exactly what they did. They were also busy throwing rocks in the higher places of the castle too.

The creatures even surprised Josiah, King Luke, and YES, even Scarecrow. They have magical powers, especially when it comes to defense. They cast spells on every knight, archer, Merman, and the towns people as well. The creatures spells can't harm others, only attack with defense. Also, they are pretty good with the sword and shield fighting against the Grave Diggers.

When it comes to fighting, the Mermen really proved it. These creatures of war certainly showed it in the battle against Scarecrow and his minions. Razor-sharp tridents, agility, stamina, and also their fast thinking of war tactics, they were nearly invincible. There shields covered their entire bodies, their armor is rock, solid hard, made from rare material which these creatures discovered. Josiah and King Luke could not believe the Mermen's performance.

Scarecrow's men were falling quickly because all of the Grave Diggers have NO fighting experience just like Scarecrow and getting really angry about this outcome. Scarecrow thought with a large number of Grave Diggers he would have won this war really easily. Even though Scarecrow's minions were well-trained, but each Grave Digger had no idea about war tactics, just like Scarecrow. So Scarecrow had to think of something QUICKLY to break the spirit of Josiah's army, if not, Scarecrow will not have an army left. That was the only advantage for Scarecrow. Still the battle raged on both sides. Scarecrow started to find Josiah, King Luke and Gobby. Soon after Scarecrow found them, all three of them, fighting off the Grave Diggers. "JOSIAH AND GOBBY", shouted Scarecrow. Both of them turned around. Scarecrow got the "Flame of Creation" and said, "Let's see if your old man likes this in his belly". Scarecrow threw the "Flame of Creation" at King Luke, in a short distance, and struck the king like Scarecrow said, right through his belly, then King Luke fell to the ground. Josiah ran to his father and said, "FATHER, NO". King Luke looked up at his son and said, "It is time for me to be with my fore-fathers. Let me go, son. Now you are the new King of Hydra, I know you will make me proud. I was so wrong about the creatures, about EVERYTHING. We shall meet again when it is your time to pass, I love you, King

Josiah". With that King Luke died in the arms of his son Josiah, but at the hands of Scarecrow.

"I am choked up with tears, ha, ha, ha". Josiah picked up the "Flame of Creation" and everyone backed up. Josiah looked at Scarecrow and said, "If I drive this blade into you, every Grave Digger DIES. If I drive this blade in tome, they follow my command". Scarecrow looked at Josiah with worry and did not realize what Scarecrow had done by throwing the "Flame of Creation" at King Luke. Josiah continued, "BUT, if I drive this blade into the ground, where EVERY Grave Digger came to life, they all die". Gobby said, "I didn't think of that Josiah, DO IT. It is a lot easier then trying to put that cursed blade in Scarecrow".

At that moment, EVERYONE stopped fighting, complete silence. Josiah said, "Hope said SOMEONE tampered with the "Flame of Creation" and I figured it out who it is". Scarecrow still looking at Josiah and very nervous looking right now. Gobby said, "Who is it then, Josiah"? Josiah turned to look at Gobby and back at Scarecrow and said, "It is my mother Sandra". "WHAT", said Gobby, "Are you sure? How can you be sure about this"? Josiah said, "My mother and I were the ONLY ones who knew about the Mermen but I didn't think they were going to aid us in this battle because they kept to themselves, and was I wrong about the Mermen, they DID aid us. This is what I am about to do Scarecrow or MOTHER, YOU and Scarecrow will have your OWN battle to fight, if you win we follow you BUT if Scarecrow wins, it is a different ball game, AGREED"?

Scarecrow just stared at Josiah and did not know what to make out of this. Gobby said, "How can you make Scarecrow fight SCARECROW"? Josiah said, "Easily, by braking the "Flame of Creation' into half. And with that, Josiah went over to the nearest Grave Digger, grabbed a club out of his hands and smashed it over the "Flame of Creation". With that, the sword cracked into half. Scarecrow screamed with pain and disappeared. Along with every Grave Digger too. Screaming with pain and the next thing every last Grave Digger was nothing but a big, huge pile of black mud. Everyone cheered and celebrated. Gobby said to Josiah, "What do you think happened to Scarecrow"? Josiah said, "They are about to fight each other where it all began, for SCARECROW, for that matter". "And where would that be"? The very place I met Jeremy Andrews, at the waterfall, close to your cottage-like-cabin, said Josiah. "We have to go there NOW, said, Gobby. "NO", said Josiah, "This is Scarecrows battle with my mother, not OTHERS. Besides we have a celebration on the way and the dead need to be buried in honor and be respected, like my father King Luke". Gobby said, "I understand. But why your mother"? Josiah turned around to look at Gobby and said, "I don't know, I am hoping the REAL Scarecrow can tell us. All I can do now is pray for his safety". "I agree with you, one hundred percent", said Gobby.

CHAPTER 30

SCARECROW CONFRONTS THE FAKE SCARECROW

Soon after Scarecrow ended up in the very place Scarecrow met Josiah (back then he called himself Stranger to hide his identity). Scarecrow said, "So, I am here AGAIN, at this waterfall". Very weak and in a lot of pain, Scarecrow felt something like he never felt before. Scarecrows body started to glow, like a golden color all-over him. Next then, the golden light left Scarecrow and when about twenty feet away from him, the golden glow of light turned into another SCARECROW, but this time it was the REAL Scarecrow.

The fake Scarecrow just looked, in complete shock, at the same time could not move because of the pain he was in because when Josiah destroyed the "Flame of Creation", half of the fake Scarecrow's soul was destroyed. After a sword appeared before both of them, right in the middle of them both was the "Flame of Creation" but in a different form, a lot different to the one in the past. It had the REAL Scarecrows face on the handle of the sword, not the fake Scarecrow.

Scarecrow walked over to the "Flame of Creation" (which is a dark blue all over, not black, red and grey strings around it either), picking up the sword at hand and said, "I don't know who you are OR where you are from but I promise you this, you demon, you will not have eyes tonight, neither ears or a tongue. There is no paths between lions and men. You will wonder the afterlife blind, deaf and dumb, the foul who thought you could kill the REAL SCARECROW".

With that Scarecrow ran towards the fake Scarecrow and drove the sword right through the fake Scarecrows body. After the fake Scarecrow fell to the ground and said, "Death is only the beginning", then disappeared into a dark, black, thick cloud of smoke. The fake Scarecrow is no more. The REAL Scarecrow defeated the leader of the Creator of the Grave Diggers and said to himself, "You weren't so strong after all".

CHAPTER 31

QUEEN SANDRA APPEARS

After the fall of the fake Scarecrow, a spirit came out of the "Flame of Creation" then said, You don't know me but I know you Scarecrow. My name is Queen Sandra, wife of King Luke. I am here to help you heal your body and soul. I have poisoned you because of my vengeance towards the leader of the creatures, Gobby. You see, my plan was to get enough information out of the creatures head leader, who was Gobby at that time, so myself and my husband would get rid of them all. I was selfish, both of us were. WE even used Gobby's brother Hope to get closer. I promised him power and riches but I killed him because of my and my husbands self-righteous power. I was so wrong about the creatures in the war. So wrong in deed, I hope you will forgive me because I used you to get back at them, you were a pawn, nothing more, you did nothing wrong, it was all ME".

Scarecrow just stared and nodded his head up and down. After Scarecrow said, "You give me ONE good reason why I should forgive you QUEEN"? "There is no reason for you to forgive me. All I can say is that people, like myself wronged you and we ALL make mistakes, we are not ALL perfect". Scarecrow said, "Fair enough then, I forgive you. But I will forgive you on one condition Sandra"? Name it, Scarecrow, " said Queen Sandra, "I will do anything to make you happy and clear my name and my husbands as well". " I want you to tell Josiah and Gobby what has happened HERE", said Scarecrow. "OK", said Queen Sandra.

After Queen Sandra said, "I forgot to mention, in order for me to heal you, you have to return to your OWN time. If not you will die because of the power from the "Flame of Creation". All that power into one body and soul is too much for one person to handle, I hope you will understand that, I am sorry. Scarecrow nodded his head again and said, "I understand. Just tell Josiah and Gobby all the best of luck and tell them both THEY are the only true friends I have".

Scarecrow paused and said after, "I remember EVERYTHING you know, all the terrible deeds you made me do". Queen Sandra said, "When I heal you and return you to your time Scarecrow, you will forget everything. You will wake up here by this waterfall and think it was all just a dream". Thank-you", said Scarecrow, "I really like that, in a sense I will forget about Josiah and the creatures". Queen Sandra smiled and said, "Well, maybe you will remember some good things". "I hope so", said Scarecrow.

Next then, Queen Sandra held up her hand and waved it at Scarecrow. Next then Scarecrow saw the same door he and Josiah walked through in the past. Scarecrow looked back and said to Queen Sandra, "Good-bye". With that, Scarecrow walked through the door and the door behind him closed and disappeared into thin air.

CHAPTER 32

JEREMY ANDREWS BACK TO HIMSELF

Soon after Jeremy opened his eyes and found himself lying on the ground next to the waterfall. Jeremy said to himself, "What a dream, I must have slipped and hit my head on the ground, but what a DREAM, so REAL, like I really thought I was there or something". Anyway Jeremy picked himself up from the ground, grab his buckets, filled them up again with water and headed home.

After Jeremy got home his mother Amber said to him, "What took you so long, if I knew you were going to take that long to get some water, I would have done it myself". "Sorry mom", said Jeremy, as he started to wash the dishes while thinking of that dream he had.

The next morning was the same for Jeremy Andrews. His father Carl asked Jeremy to help him out in the field farming. While working, Jeremy could not stop thinking of that dream he had. In the afternoon, his mother asked him to get more water from the waterfall. And again Jeremy got the two big water buckets at hand and headed over to the waterfall. When Jeremy got there, he saw something really big, like on old chest or something. Jeremy put down the water buckets and went over to the old chest. On the chest there was a letter and it said, "To my dearest friend, I hope you are well. My mother Sandra told me the entire story and I am sorry what you went through. In return I have included a map for a ultimate reward for you. I wish I could see you on last time. Sandra and the others, in the afterlife, send this chest over to you here with all their power combined. I hope you will like the reward, I know you will. Also, Gobby would like to say hi to you as well and wish you all the best of luck, your friend, King Josiah".

Jeremy could not believe what he had read. "I KNEW it was not a dream, it was all REAL". After Jeremy opened the old chest and to Jeremy's surprise there was a crown, scepter and very fine material clothing and a cape. Jeremy got the map out and read it carefully and it said, "Go behind to a underground tunnel which will lead to your ultimate reward". With that, Jeremy close the old chest, put it underneath his arm and in the other hand was the map. Off Jeremy went to the secret tunnel, behind the Kingdom of Hydra.

CHAPTER 33

THE ULTIMATE REWARD

The castle and to where Jeremy lived was about two and a half to three hours away. When Jeremy got to the Kingdom of Hydra, Jeremy did what the map said. After Jeremy went around the castle, he saw unusual hand writing. Jeremy went over to get a closer look and it said, "Dear Scarecrow, your ultimate reward is down this tunnel, all you have to do is slide the rock over to the left and head straight down". So Jeremy did what the message asked of him. Jeremy slide the rock to the left side and sure-enough, there was a tunnel and it headed straight down.

As Jeremy walked down the tunnel, he saw a glowing blue light ahead. As Jeremy got closer, he could not believe his eyes, it was the "Flame of Creation". Jeremy picked up the sword and said, "This must be the ultimate reward". "Not exactly, King Scarecrow", said a voice. Jeremy turned around and it was one of the Mermen. After the Merman said that, the "Flame of Creation" glowed even brighter. Soon Jeremy felt a change in his body and in about a few minutes later, Jeremy was no longer Jeremy, he was Scarecrow once again.

"Josiah is right about one thing Merman", said Scarecrow. "And what is that, my Lord"? "He said at the end of the day I will want to be "Scarecrow" again". After saying that, both Scarecrow and the Merman laughed. The Merman said, "Follow me, my Lord, everyone is waiting for you". So Scarecrow followed the Merman until they entered a very large lake where there were hundreds of Mermen, as if they were excepting Scarecrow. They told Scarecrow that he is the new King, appointed by Josiah by the history records which the Mermen keep track of. There was gold and silver everywhere and Scarecrow is the King to every Merman around him.

Scarecrow later said, "What about the creatures? Do they interact with the humans now?". One of the Merman said, "OH YES, my Lord. They get along with them fine". "That's good to hear", said Scarecrow, smiling. With everything said and done, the Mermen celebrated and welcomed their new King, King Scarecrow of the Mermen. The rest is history...... Scarecrow never married and lived a great life with the Mermen. Scarecrow was buried with the other Kings and Queens like King Josiah, King Luke, King Gobby and many others. With the power of the "Flame of Creation", Scarecrow remembers EVERYTHING, all the terrible deeds he has caused and done, making the Grave Diggers, the weapon making, killing a lot of creatures in the process. Scarecrow could not get rid of his demons of what he has done in the past but one thing is for sure and Gobby's brother Hope was right..... Scarecrow was the CHOSEN ONE, he reunited both creatures, Mermen and humans together and at the end of all things......it paid off.....with the help of Queen Sandra and she didn't know she was helping either at that time.....funny how life works like that.

To be Continued

9 781953 537430